Je
Geo
c. 14

LINDSAY BARRETT GEORGE

In the Garden:
Who's Been Here?

Greenwillow Books

An Imprint of HarperCollinsPublishers

It is lightly drizzling on this summer morning.
"Christina, please take Jeremy into the garden
and pick some vegetables.
I'm still baking."
"But Mom, it's raining."
"Don't worry, you won't melt,"
Christina's mother says.
"And please put Sonny outside."

Christina and her brother take a bucket
out of the toolshed
and walk over to the garden.
Something brown streaks across the yard.
"Christina . . . a bunny," Jeremy whispers,
pointing toward the garden gate.
"They're cute, Jeremy, but bunnies
eat anything that's green in the garden."

In a few minutes, it stops drizzling.
Raindrops cling to the poppies.
A visitor darts from blossom to blossom,
sucking nectar from the flowers.

Christina looks down
into a large sunflower.

"Something's been eating the seeds
in the middle of this sunflower.
I wonder . . .

"Who's been here?"

A chipmunk.

Christina walks down a row of tomato plants.
"This one looks good," she says,
bending to pick a tomato.

Sonny looks at it, too.

"I'll pick you another one, Sonny.
This is for Mom," she says.

"Christina," Jeremy says,
looking closely at a tomato plant.
"Part of this leaf is gone."

Who's been here?

A tomato hornworm.

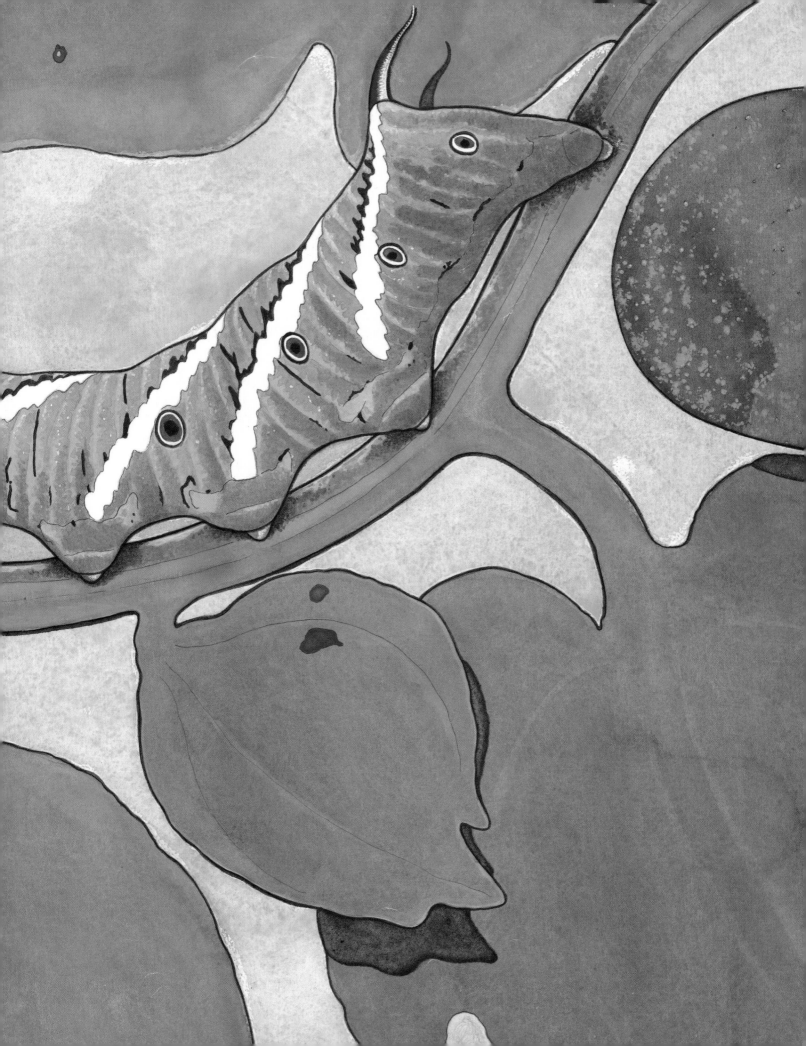

Jeremy picks some lettuce.

"Somebody's already had dinner,"
Christina says, standing over
some nibbled greens.

"I know who was hungry,"
Jeremy says.

Who's been here?

A cottontail rabbit.

Christina crouches down
and picks a large cucumber
from the patch.

"Hey Sonny, don't step on the cucumbers,"
Christina says.

"Jeremy, come over here
and look at this leaf."

Her brother runs his finger along the shiny line.
The line stops in the middle of the leaf.
"It's slimy," he says.

Who's been here?

A slug.

They pick some ears of corn
and drop them into the bucket.

"Christina," Jeremy says,
"I see a brown and yellow snake."

"Leave it alone, Jeremy. . . .
It's probably a garter,
and they're not very friendly."

Christina does not notice
that the husks on an ear of corn
have been shredded.

The insides of some of the kernels
have been pecked out.

Who's been here?

A crow.

Jeremy reaches up and snaps beans off their vines.
"These are sweet."

As Christina helps him gather beans,
she wonders out loud.
"Look at this empty space.
What happened to the plants?"

Who's been here?

A deer mouse.

"I'm hungry," Christina says,
  and she sits down in the garden.

"Let's eat this carrot," Jeremy says.

"Look at that carrot top,"
  Christina says.

"Someone cut it," her brother says.

"It hasn't been cut off . . . ,"
  Christina realizes.
"It's been chewed off."

  Who's been here?

A woodchuck.

"Jeremy, I think we have enough vegetables
for *two* dinners!" Christina says.

The children pick hollyhocks
for their mother.

"Christina," Jeremy whispers,
and points to a hole in the ground.

Who's been here?

A mole.

Jeremy and his sister walk back
to the house with a bucket filled
with vegetables and flowers.

"Race you, Sonny," Jeremy yells.

"Watch me, Jeremy.
I can do a headstand."

Jeremy stops at the peach tree.
Someone has left three plates
and a pitcher of milk
on the table.

Sonny wags his tail.

Jeremy looks around and wonders . . .

"Who's been here?"

The **chipmunk** is a small member of the squirrel family. It eats seeds, nuts, and fruits. A chipmunk will save some of its food by stuffing it into its cheeks and storing it in underground tunnels. Chipmunks are good climbers and can jump from one sunflower stalk to the next in search of seeds.

The **crow** is one of America's best-known birds. Its feathers are coal black and it has a distinctive call—"caw, caw." Crows often live near people and are very smart and shrewd. They eat many kinds of vegetables, but their favorite food is corn.

The **tomato hornworm** is a large green or brownish caterpillar with a hornlike structure at the end of its body. It usually feeds on the leaves of tomato plants. The hornworm hatches from eggs that are laid on the underside of leaves. When it's fully grown, it burrows into the ground and forms a cocoon. It emerges from the soil as a moth.

The **deer mouse** is the most common mammal in North America, living in every type of habitat. It has a very good sense of smell, which makes it an expert at digging up buried seeds. The deer mouse eats mostly seeds but will also eat acorns, fruits, insects, fungi, and some green vegetation.

The **cottontail rabbit** is one of the most common garden visitors. It eats lettuce, peas, beans, flowers, clover, and the tender bark of trees. The cottontail lives in a tunnel system called a warren and stays close to its home area when searching for food.

The **woodchuck**, also known as the groundhog, creates large underground tunnel systems under open fields and meadows. You can also find the woodchuck in backyards, especially those with vegetable gardens. A single woodchuck can do a lot of damage to a garden's vegetation, especially carrot tops, peas, beans, clover, and grasses.

The **slug** is a close relative of the snail, but it has no shell. Like the snail, it has eyes on tentacles above its head. The slug leaves a slime trail when traveling over plants and paths. It eats plants, especially young ones. Its mouth works like a rasp to cut into plants.

Moles are little mammals that are rarely seen. They burrow down in the earth, and eat earthworms and insects. The burrows they dig help mix air into the soil, but sometimes these air pockets can harm or dislodge the roots of plants. Mice may also use the mole tunnels to find and eat the roots and bulbs of garden plants.

For Will

In the Garden: Who's Been Here? Copyright © 2006 by Lindsay Barrett George. All rights reserved. Manufactured in China. www.harperchildrens.com

Watercolors and inks were used to prepare the full-color art. The text type is Albertina.

Library of Congress Cataloging-in-Publication Data: George, Lindsay Barrett. In the garden: who's been here? / by Lindsay Barrett George.   p.   cm.   "Greenwillow Books." Summary: As Jeremy and Christina pick vegetables for their mother, they see evidence of animals and insects that have been in the garden before them. ISBN-10: 0-06-078762-7 (trade bdg.). ISBN-13: 978-0-06-078762-2 (trade bdg.). ISBN-10: 0-06-078763-5 (lib. bdg.) ISBN-13: 978-0-06-078763-9 (lib. bdg.) [1. Gardens—Fiction. 2. Garden animals—Fiction. I. Animals—Habits and behavior—Fiction.] I. Title. PZ7.G29334Img 1995 [E]—dc22 2005040347

First Edition 10 9 8 7 6 5 4

 Greenwillow Books